Weekly Reader Books presents

THE FIREBALL MYSTERY

The
Fireball Mystery

by
MARY ADRIAN

Illustrated by Reisie Lonette

HASTINGS HOUSE, PUBLISHERS

New York

Library of Congress Cataloging in Publication Data

Adrian, Mary   The fireball mystery.

SUMMARY: Three children hunt for a meteorite they saw fall from outer space but run into some unexpected complications.
[1. Mystery and detective stories]   I. Lonette, Reisie.   II. Title.
PZ7.A26183Fi   [Fic]   77-17151
ISBN 0-8038-2325-8

Printed in the United States of America

This book is a presentation of Weekly Reader Books.
Weekly Reader Books offers book clubs for children from preschool to young adulthood. All quality hardcover books are selected by a distinguished Weekly Reader Selection Board.

For further information write to:
  Weekly Reader Books
  1250 Fairwood Ave.
  Columbus, Ohio 43216

Contents

CHAPTER ONE

The Mysterious Lights

TIM SWITCHED on the light in his room, tumbled out of bed, and with arms resting on the windowsill, looked out at the dark river. He was spending his first night in his new home—a floating house resting on logs anchored to pilings along the river-front.

Tim was thrilled with the idea of living in a different kind of house. Especially since they had bought the island just across the river. Dad said in five years the land would be worth twice as much. Then he might think of selling it. But until then—

Until then, the island was theirs. And Dad said it would be perfect for stargazing.

The trouble was, Tim dreaded going over there. As he stared at the island, a long strip of land with trees towering toward the starlit sky, a cold shiver ran through him. Tim had a secret that he shared with no one, not even with his sister, Vicki, who was nine—two years younger than he was.

He was afraid of the dark.

Lots of times Tim had stargazed from the front lawn of their old home with his dad. It was clear enough to see lots of stars and he had felt safe there. But to stargaze from an island, a big dark island, with only his sister for company, would be a different matter.

If Dad had not had to go away on business, he could have counted on him to come along. But Dad's last words to Tim and Vicki were, "That island should be a great place to see some of the planets. Why, you might even spot a comet."

Dad's words were ringing in Tim's ears. A comet! Boy! He'd sure like to see one. How could he wait a week or two for Dad to come back? But that island—it would be really dark there tomorrow night.

Tim was about to go back to bed when he saw lights blink on the island. That was strange. What was a person doing on their property in the middle of the night?

Just then someone nudged Tim in the ribs and said in a loud whisper, "Boo!"

Tim jumped and glared at his sister.

Vicki put her hand over her mouth to stifle a giggle.

"Very funny," Tim whispered.

"I'm sorry," Vicki answered. Then she grinned, a wide grin that showed the braces on her front teeth. "I just had to. Move over," she added. She squeezed next to Tim and looked out at the river. "I couldn't sleep! I'm so excited!"

"Do you see what I see on the island?" Tim asked her.

"Hey!" whispered Vicki. "Somebody is flashing different colored lights. They've gone out now. There they are again. That's funny. Who do you suppose is on our island? And what's he doing?"

Tim shrugged. "I wish I knew."

Vicki cupped her chin in her hands. "Dad said there was an old house on the island. Maybe somebody's poking around over there." Her eyes grew wide.

"Uh-oh," Tim sighed. "Here she goes again."

But Vicki was lost in her daydream and didn't seem to notice her brother.

"It could be a real mystery." She plucked excitedly at his pajama sleeve, "And we can go investigate tomorrow night when we stargaze!"

"Tomorrow night!" Tim drew back. "What's wrong with the daytime?"

"We have to *investigate*, silly."

"What's to investigate?" he asked, a little nervously.

"Everything! We can spy around that old house, for one." She peered out at the dark strip of land. "Those

10

lights are gone now. I can't see a thing. I wonder what the island looks like? Do you think there's lots of animals? Or maybe a cave? What do you think?"

Tim shrugged. "I guess we'll find out," he answered, thinking, "And she'll probably find out I'm afraid of the dark!"

Vicki sighed and laid her head against her brother's arm. "I'm getting sleepy now," she yawned.

They waited. All was quiet except for the river lapping against the front of the floating house. Suddenly they heard a sound from the next room.

"I hope I didn't wake Mom," Vicki whispered. "I'd better go."

She tiptoed out of the room. Tim watched the mysterious lights until finally they stopped blinking and the blackness of night made the island look like a long, dark shadow. Then he slipped back into bed.

The next morning the children forgot about the strange lights on the island. They were too excited about exploring their new home. They couldn't wait to get out and look around. They did their chores as quickly as they could and dashed out the door.

Tim and Vicki ran across a small, wooden bridge onto the dock where their dad had left a canoe for their use. It was an old canoe, but Tim was eager to paddle to the island. After all, it was daytime now, and there was nothing to be afraid of.

Or was there? Tim suddenly remembered the mysterious lights.

11

Just then a boy about his own age, with dark brown hair and glasses, came onto the dock, marched up to them, took a deep breath and said,

"Hi, I'm Joey Baker and you're the new kids. Mom told me you were coming. I live three houses down in a house like yours. There are ten floating houses here, but hardly any other kids so I'm really glad you moved here." He put his hands in his pockets and beamed at them.

Vicki was smiling back, but Tim blinked in surprise. Never in all his life had he heard anyone talk so fast and wave his arms at the same time. And he wondered what was making the front of Joey's shirt move up and down.

Suddenly a head peeked out of Joey's red striped shirt—a head with unwinking eyes and a flickering forked tongue.

"A snake!" shrieked Vicki.

Joey proudly pulled out his pet and swung him over his shoulders. Both Tim and Vicki took a few quick steps back.

"Don't worry!" Joey laughed. "Bobo is a harmless garter snake. I found him this spring. Dad doesn't like snakes in the house, so I built a wooden cage with a window in one side for Bobo. We put in dirt and weeds and some flat stones. I feed Bobo worms. In the fall I'll turn him loose so he can hibernate like other snakes in the winter."

Tim was impressed, but Vicki knew she wouldn't

12

want a snake for a pet. She backed away when Joey came closer and said, "Bobo feels with his tongue. He won't mind if you touch him."

"Well *I* would!" Vicki shuddered.

"I've touched snakes," said Tim. "They're not dirty or slimy the way some people think."

"You're right." Joey fondled Bobo and let the snake crawl along his arm. "You've got to handle Bobo gently, though. Otherwise he'll give off an awful smelly liquid from a gland near his tail. All garter snakes do that."

"Yuck," Vicki said. "Why don't you get a cat or a dog?"

Joey grinned. "I like creeping, crawling creatures. I like all kinds of animals and I like to spy on them at night. There are lots of them on the island, but I can't go there anymore because your dad has no trespassing signs all over the place." Without a breath he added, "Of course, I guess I could go with you."

"Are there really lots of animals there?" Vicki asked.

"You bet! Owls, raccoons, deer—you name it! I could show you all kinds of things."

"Sure," Vicki answered. "We can all go to the island. We're going to stargaze there tonight. Tim has a telescope. We saw . . ."

Vicki did not finish, for just then a blond teen-aged boy came up and slapped Joey on the back.

"Hi, Joey. How are you doing?"

Joey turned around and looked up at the tall boy

13

in faded jeans and a blue shirt. "Hi, Skipper. These are the kids who just moved here. Mom told me their names. This is Tim Andrews and his sister Vicki."

"Welcome to our floating colony," said Skipper. He turned to another teen-ager, a short, dark-haired boy. "This is my cousin, Ronnie. He's spending the summer with us."

"Yeah, I know," said Joey eagerly. "My mom found out from your mom."

Skipper shook his head and laughed. "Joey Baker, you know everything that goes on around here. But I'll bet you didn't see the lights on the island last night."

"No, I didn't," answered Joey, looking surprised.

Skipper folded his arms around himself and looked very fearful. He leaned forward and said in a loud whisper, "They were very spooky lights. They went off and then came on. And . . ."

Tim had found his voice. "I saw those lights!"

"So did I," echoed Vicki. "And we're going over there tonight. Tim wants to stargaze," she added proudly.

"So you want to stargaze from the island!" Skipper said. "Good for you. Maybe you'll find out who was there last night. Those lights looked very creepy. Didn't they, Ronnie?"

His cousin nodded. "They sure did. I don't think I'd want to be on that island at night." He turned to Skipper. "How about getting our fishing tackle and see what we can catch in the river?"

14

"Hey, that's a good idea," Skipper answered. "I'd like to scoot around in my boat, anyway. So long, kids. See you later."

Three solemn faces watched the two teen-agers hurry along the dock and cross the wooden bridge to Skipper's floating house.

Finally Joey broke the silence. "I'm going to put Bobo back in his cage. Then I'm all for going to the island and doing some sleuthing."

Tim swallowed hard and shifted from one foot to the other.

Joey looked at him, puzzled. "What's the matter? You're going to stargaze there tonight, aren't you?"

"Sure," Tim replied hesitantly. He was wondering how he could keep Joey from finding out he was afraid of the dark.

"Well," Joey persisted. "Don't you want to look for clues on the island and see who was there?"

Before Tim could answer, Vicki took him by the arm and started pulling him toward their canoe. "Of course you do! You're not going back to look at your star books all day!"

Vicki stumbled getting into the canoe, almost losing her footing, and nearly tipping it over. She just grabbed the sides in time.

"Hurry up!" she cried, pulling the paddles from under the seats.

She could hardly wait to get to the island. The island and the mysterious lights.

CHAPTER TWO

The Fireball

"LET ME sit in the stern," Tim said, taking a paddle from Vicki and making his way carefully past her. When he had seated himself, Joey climbed in, took the other paddle and they set off, stopping every so often to watch gulls gliding by.

"I've rowed my dad's boat to the island," Joey said, "but it's an old tub and you've got to pull on the oars for all you're worth. This canoe is great."

They had to paddle quickly to get out of the way of an approaching yellow and green motorboat. It sped swiftly over the blue water, motor purring smoothly. A red-haired man waved to the children as his boat passed by.

Vicki and the boys waved back and shouted, "Hi."

"Who's that?" Vicki asked Joey.

"I've never seen him around before," Joey replied. "He must be here on vacation."

Their canoe was swaying from the ripples made by the motorboat.

"Hey, this is fun," Vicki exclaimed. Holding on to the rim of the canoe and grinning, she rocked it more.

"It would be great if we capsized," Tim scowled. "Why don't you sit still, or else trade places with Joey and do some paddling yourself?"

"All right," Vicki agreed and cautiously changed seats with Joey.

Joey settled back into his seat and said teasingly, "The river's nice for swimming Vicki, but not out in the middle. It's great about a mile down the shore. You two should probably paddle to the sandbar on the far side of the island. It's the best place to come ashore."

Both Tim's and Vicki's arms were tired from paddling, and they were glad to reach the island. With the help of Joey and Vicki, Tim pulled the canoe up on shore and tied it securely to a tree. They looked around for clues on the sandbar, but there were no footprints to show that anyone had been there.

"Well," Joey remarked, "the tide could have washed away any footprints. Besides, we've got lots of other places to look. I know every shortcut and trail on this island. So let's inspect the marsh and see if anyone was there."

Joey led the way along a path through the woods, and soon they came to a marsh—a small treeless tract of soft wet land with an open space of shallow water. Blackbirds called from the cattails along the shoreline, and a mallard duck led her family in and around the rushes.

The children immediately searched the marsh for some clues. But once again they saw no evidence that anyone had been there.

Joey was not discouraged, though. "Maybe the lights you saw came from the old house," he said. "It's not far. Let's take a look."

Tim and Vicki followed Joey through a grove of trees and before too long an old one-story house with a moss-covered roof came into view.

The children peered in the windows. But all that met their eyes were empty rooms with dust on the floors.

Then Joey tried to open the front door. "I might have known it would be locked," he announced. "Every time I've tried to get into this house, I couldn't budge this door. Anyway, it doesn't look as if anyone has been here for ages."

"It sure doesn't," Tim agreed. He looked at the open area in front of the old house. "This would be a good place to stargaze from," he said. Then he wondered how he was going to face the dark that night. He dreaded it, and he was sure Joey would make fun of him if he found out he was scared.

Tim's thoughts were suddenly interrupted when he heard Joey say, "You know something? Those strange lights have me stumped. We haven't found one single clue. It sure is a mystery."

Vicki's face lit up. "I love mysteries!"

That evening when the children returned to the island they talked about the mysterious lights as they sat Indian fashion on the ground in front of the old house. They were waiting for it to get dark so that they could stargaze. But every few minutes Tim looked around uneasily—in back and on both sides of him.

"You sure are jittery," remarked Joey.

Tim didn't answer.

Joey shrugged, got up and walked over to a tree on the edge of the clearing. He motioned for Tim and Vicki to come.

"Look what I found," he said, displaying two small brown objects in the palm of his hand. "These are pellets from a great horned owl." He pulled out a pocket knife from his jeans and carefully sliced one open. Out popped a miniature skull, white as ivory.

"What on earth is that?" asked Tim, wide-eyed with curiosity.

"It's probably the skull of a blue jay," Joey answered. "You can tell it's a bird's skull because it has a beak and no teeth. You see, an owl catches its prey with its claws and swallows it whole, but it can't digest the feathers or the bones or fur. Something in its stomach turns the undigested food into pellets. Then the owl spits them up. They're clean and dry."

Tim was amazed and Vicki demanded that Joey slice open the other pellet right away. Joey happily obliged and announced that the skull in the second pellet belonged to a meadow mouse. "See the two long front teeth and the heavy, wide skull?"

"Wow!" exclaimed Tim. "You're like a detective, Joey."

Joey grinned with pleasure. "After we've stargazed, I hope a great horned owl shows up. He eats small animals, and he's so much fun to watch. When he hoots at night it sounds really weird!" Joey looked around. "It won't be long now before dark."

The full moon gave off plenty of light as night descended on the island. The wild creatures started to come out of hiding, cautiously. The children couldn't see them, but they heard them. The stillness was broken by the sounds of cracking twigs and rustling leaves.

Joey pointed out a rabbit hopping along the edge of the clearing.

"I hope no owl catches that rabbit," Vicki whispered.

Nervous, Tim looked in all directions. He had mounted his telescope on his tripod, but he made no effort to stargaze.

Joey stared at him with a puzzled expression.

"What's the matter? Are you afraid of the dark?"

"Of course I'm not afraid of the dark," snapped Tim.

Reluctantly he focused his telescope on the sky. As he looked through it, Joey drew close. "Tell me what you're seeing," he said. "Is it that big star over there?"

"Yeah. But that's no star. It's a planet. Venus. It looks like a star because it reflects the sun's light. You know, the way the moon does. Here, take a look."

Joey took the telescope. "Do you know anything else about Venus?" he asked.

"Sure," Tim answered, grinning because he'd done a five page report on the planets the past year in school. "Venus is our nearest neighbor. That's why it's called the earth's sister. There are nine planets in our solar system. Mercury, Venus, Earth, Mars, Jupiter, Saturn, Uranus, Neptune and Pluto."

Vicki joined in, "And you know what? People used to think there was life on Venus, but now they know it's too hot for people to live there." She looked away dreamily. "That's probably why a lot of people think flying saucers come from Mars instead. It's cooler on Mars. But I heard the other day that flying saucers come from solar systems so far away you can't even see them with Tim's telescope!"

"I'll tell you what you *can* see," Tim said. "Look close and you'll see some of Jupiter's moons. Jupiter's the 'giant.' It's got twelve moons. They're satellites of Jupiter."

21

"I get it," Joey said as he gazed through the telescope. "It's the same as our moon, only Jupiter has twelve, and I can see four of them right now."

He turned to Vicki. "Don't you want to see?"

"Sure. But I'm not so interested in planets. I like to look for spaceships."

"You never see any, though," Tim said. "And I see plenty of stuff."

Vicki looked away from the telescope and raised her eyebrows. "I haven't seen any *so far*."

Tim took over, focusing the telescope towards the west while Joey and Vicki waited. The deep croaking of a bullfrog sounded across the silent marsh. Joey croaked back. He even hooted like a great horned owl, hoping to get an answer, but only silence greeted him, and soon he grew restless.

Breathing in Tim's ear, he said, "Stop keeping us in suspense. What do you see now?"

"Don't be so impatient," said Tim. "I'm looking at the Big Dipper. You can see it very clearly—the bowl and the handle."

Vicki had seen the Big Dipper many times through Tim's telescope. In fact, she could see it right now with her naked eye. So she let Joey take a turn.

Joey was surprised at how distinctly he could see the seven stars of the Big Dipper.

"Take a look at the Little Dipper," said Tim. "It's above the Big Dipper. See the big star at the end of the Little Dipper's handle?"

23

Joey looked real hard. "Yeah. I see it."

"That's Polaris, the North Star," Tim explained. "When you see Polaris, you know the direction is north. That's good to know in case you get lost. The Big Dipper is only part of a constellation called the Big Bear."

"Hey, take it easy," said Joey. "What's a constellation?"

Tim laughed. "I'll give you a copy of my stargazing list. I call it that, but it really isn't just about the stars. I put in the planets and other things I found out about outer space."

"I put in stuff, too." Vicki said. "About flying saucers and space travel."

"Great," replied Joey. "But what's a constellation?"

"It's a group of stars. If you look close you can see how the other stars around the Big Dipper form the head and legs of the Great Bear." Tim also pointed out to Joey a constellation called Leo, the Lion, and another called Scorpius. In fact, he was so busy explaining things to Joey that he forgot about its being dark.

Suddenly Tim realized that he wasn't afraid. Why, he had expected to be scared out of his wits, but here he was on a big, strange island—in the dark, with animals all about and a whole river between himself and home—and enjoying it! For the first time in his life he faced the dark without visions of strangers or animals attacking him.

24

"What is it?" Joey asked, because Tim had stopped talking and was lost in thought.

"Oh," he started. "Nothing much. I was just thinking." He turned and grinned at Joey and began pointing out another constellation.

All this while, Vicki had been deep in her own daydreams. She pictured herself rocketing through space in a silver-winged spaceship, visiting all the planets. Tim would come, too, and maybe Joey. They would go so far they would be able to meet all kinds of people from outer space.

"There's a shooting star!" she cried, forgetting her daydreams in her excitement. She jumped up and down and squealed, "Now I can make a wish and it will come true." And she knew just what she'd wish for! She stood perfectly still, squeezed her eyes shut, and concentrated with all her might.

"Maybe it will," Tim said, "But that's a meteor. Sometimes people call a meteor a shooting star, but it's really not a star."

"What's a meteor?" Joey inquired.

"It's a chunk of a planet that gets knocked off and flies through space," Tim explained. "A lot of meteors are no bigger than peas. And most of them burn up when they hit the earth's atmosphere."

"You mean like that?" Joey pointed to a brilliant ball of fire streaking through the sky.

Tim nodded, open-mouthed, and Vicki stared in

25

a trance at the glowing streak. The fiery ball seemed to be heading straight for them.

Joey froze. "The fireball's going to hit us!" he yelled.

Vicki blinked, shoved her brother and Joey and yelled, "Let's get out of here!"

They ran back along the path, Joey now in the lead, the beam of his flashlight zigzagging as he rushed along the shortcut to the sandbar.

The next thing they knew, there was a roaring sound behind them, like an airplane going into a nosedive. Then came a sharp crackling noise and a loud thump.

"Oh no!" Joey panted. "What if it explodes?"

They kept on running until they reached the canoe, and pushing it into the water, they hopped in. Tim and Joey grabbed the paddles and headed toward the lights on shore.

"That was a narrow escape," breathed Joey. "I was sure that meteor was going to kill us."

"I was too," Tim admitted.

They paddled in silence along the smooth, inky water.

Tim sighed. He was beginning to calm down. "I've read about things like that, but I never thought it would happen to *me!* I read about a nine pound meteorite crashing through the roof of a house. It hit a woman lying on her couch and almost killed her."

"How big do you think this one was?" Joey questioned.

"I don't know," Tim replied. "But it was pretty loud. It could be big. The biggest meteorite found in the United States weighed 31,000 pounds."

"What's the difference between a meteor and a meteorite? Is a meteorite smaller?"

"No," Tim said. "After a meteor lands they call it a meteorite. I don't know why—" he stopped and his face lit up. "That meteorite landed on our property. That means it's ours! Tomorrow we can go look for it."

Then he thought of something else. He frowned, sat up straight and stopped paddling.

"What's the matter?" asked Joey, looking at his friend in alarm.

"Suppose someone else saw it land? If he finds it before we do, we're sunk."

"Is a meteorite valuable?"

"It sure is. Scientists love to get their hands on one. I hope we can find it."

Vicki said, "Now don't worry, Tim. We'll get up real early and go to the island, and we'll find it. I know we will."

Tim half smiled. He wished he could believe his sister, but he had his doubts.

CHAPTER THREE

The Stranger

AS TIM WAS getting ready for bed that night, he suddenly realized that he had left his telescope on the island. It was too late to go back there now and get it. But what if someone was already looking for the meteorite and saw his telescope and made off with it? He bit his bottom lip, and his eyes welled up with tears.

Tim stood at his window and gazed out at the island. The river was especially calm, and the moon was a white disc on the water. Well, he thought, it was no use worrying. Chances were that no one would take it. He shook his head. Besides, he couldn't do a thing until morning. He got into bed and was soon asleep.

Early the next morning the three of them set out

once again for the island. The river was as smooth as a mirror and sparkled like a diamond in the sunlight.

"That boat looks like the yellow and green one we saw yesterday," Tim remarked, pointing to a motorboat moored along the island's sandbar.

"It is," said Joey, squinting to get a better look. "The same red-haired man is sitting in the boat. I wonder what he's doing."

All at once Tim started paddling furiously.

"What's up?" Joey cried, trying to keep up with him.

"That guy with the red hair! I'll bet he's found the meteorite!"

"You could be right," Joey admitted.

Tim began to paddle for all he was worth, and Joey found himself missing strokes. As they neared the sandbar, the red-haired man waved wildly and beckoned for them to come closer.

"We'd better find out what he wants," Joey advised, breathlessly. "Besides, if we get real close, we'll be able to see if he has the meteorite in his boat."

Tim made quick splashes in the water with the paddle. Before long his canoe was alongside the stranger's boat.

"Am I glad to see you!" exclaimed the red-haired man, mopping his brow with a handkerchief. "My motor conked out. Would you go and get help for me at the marina? I have no oars with me. This is the first time I've had motor trouble."

Vicki looked at the two fishing rods and bait in the boat, but that was all she could see. "We'll be glad to go to the marina for you, won't we, Tim?"

"Sure, sure," he answered, straining his neck to see what was in the boat.

Joey leaned over and almost lost his balance, but caught himself in time. "Have you been on the island?" he asked the man.

"Not recently," he answered. "Say, you kids aren't going to let me down, are you? I need someone to tow me in as soon as possible. I'm supposed to meet a friend."

"We'll go right away," said Tim. He paddled as fast as he could.

"I guess we were wrong about him," said Vicki.

"It looks that way," answered Tim. "How far is it to the marina, Joey?"

"It's quite a distance," he replied. "Vicki, why don't you let me paddle for a while?"

Sighing wearily, Tim and Joey paddled toward the marina at the end of the long dock of floating houses.

An old man was fishing from the front deck of a floating house with his feet propped up on the railing. He waved to Joey.

They brought the canoe close to the floating house. "Hi, Sam," Joey said. "Caught any fish?"

Sam shook his head. "Not a solitary one. I'll bet you've been exploring on the island. Did you see any tigers?"

The children laughed.

"We were stargazing there last night," Vicki said.

"I saw you heading out with a telescope," said Sam. "Did you have any luck?"

Vicki nodded. "We even saw . . ." She was on the verge of telling about the meteorite, but she saw Tim's scowl and caught herself in time.

"I'll bet you saw a white elephant!" finished Sam.

"Well, not exactly." Vicki clasped and unclasped her hands nervously. "It was . . . Uh . . ."

"It's a secret," said Sam.

Vicki was relieved. "Yes. It's a secret."

Just then a tall thin man with dark hair came on the deck of Sam's floating house. He wore a short-sleeved shirt with official looking patches. Joey whispered, "That's Sheriff Williams."

"Hi, Joey," the sheriff said. "What are you up to today? I hope you're not going near the soft drink machine."

Joey looked serious. "No, sir! I'm staying away from it." He turned to Vicki and Tim. "He's talking about last week when the machine wouldn't give me a bottle of pop. So I went after my money. I stuck my arm in the machine up to my elbow."

"You did!" exclaimed Tim. "How did you get it out?"

"I didn't," Joey answered. "It took Sheriff Williams, the vending machine man and a fireman an hour to get my arm free. But I got my 15 cents back."

31

"Who are your friends, Joey?" the Sheriff asked.

Joey introduced them. "Tim and Vicki just moved here."

"Oh *that's* right. Your dad bought the island, didn't he?"

"He sure did," Tim said proudly.

"Hey, you don't look like a sheriff," Vicki spoke up. "Where's your gun and your big hat?"

Sheriff Williams laughed. "You think I need my gun around you three? Are you dangerous gangsters?"

"You bet they are," Sam told him. "Joey and his pals have been stargazing on the island. They've been hunting wild animals, too, and they're keeping something else a secret."

"A secret, eh!" said Sheriff Williams. "I'd *better* keep an eye on you young ones."

Suddenly Sam's fishing rod began to jerk and in a few seconds he pulled in a fish.

"Say! That's a big one," remarked Sheriff Williams, examining the fish. "I guess I'll go and get my fishing rod and see what luck I have."

Joey put his hand to his cheek and groaned. "I just remembered we were going to the marina to get help for a red-haired man. The engine conked out on his motorboat."

"Well, he's going to be awfully mad at you," said Sam.

Joey looked concerned. "We're going!" he said and

they paddled as fast as they could the rest of the way to the marina. It was owned by Fred Emmett, a short, stocky man with a moustache that curled at the ends.

He immediately came over to the children. "What's on your mind, Joey?"

Joey told him rapidly, as always.

"I'm glad I'm not busy now," said Fred when Joey had finished. "I'll go right away." He turned to his assistant, a teen-ager with long black hair. "You take over while I'm gone."

Vicki and the boys watched Fred take off in a motorboat and head for the island. Then they followed, but after they had gone a short distance, they were surprised to see Fred returning alone.

He swung his boat around and eased alongside them. "Did you say the man was stranded along the sandbar on the island?"

"That's right, Fred," Joey replied, puzzled.

"He's not there now." Fred scowled. "Joey Baker, are you playing a trick on me?"

"Oh, no, Fred. Honest, there was a big red-haired guy there in a yellow and green motorboat. We talked to him. Didn't we, Tim?"

"We sure did. He wanted us to hurry and get help."

"And I'll bet you took your time," said Fred, appearing annoyed.

"We did stop and talk to Sam and Sheriff Williams," Joey admitted with a sheepish expression.

Fred shook his head. "I'd better get back to the marina." With that he was off, his motor putting softly.

The children stared at each other, speechless. No man! No motorboat!

Then Joey leaned forward and said suspiciously, "Do you suppose the man wanted to sidetrack us? Maybe he found the meteorite. He probably knows that your dad owns the island and that the meteorite belongs to you."

Seeing Tim's worried look, he added, "I'm probably getting carried away. Don't pay any attention to me."

"No, you aren't," Tim muttered.

Vicki looked up at her brother. She said firmly, "Well, if we don't find the meteorite soon, that red-haired man will be suspect number one."

CHAPTER FOUR

The Missing Telescope

VICKI TOOK OVER for Joey and helped Tim paddle the rest of the way to the island. After they had carried the canoe ashore, they hurried to the open area in front of the old house. There they found the tripod but Tim's telescope was nowhere in sight.

"I knew someone would take my telescope!" wailed Tim. "I'll bet it's that guy with the red hair, and he's found the meteorite, too." Tim blinked hard to keep back the tears.

Vicki looked at her brother sympathetically.

"We haven't even looked for the meteorite," protested Joey. "So how do you know anybody found it? There's no reason to give up. I think we'll find it *and* your telescope."

Tim perked up, and looked at his friend gratefully. "I guess you're right, Joey."

"Let's look for the meteorite first," Joey said. "You can always buy another telescope, but a meteorite doesn't fall on an island every day." He shoved his hands in his pockets. "We'll cover every inch of this island," he said in a determined voice. "The crash sounded as if it was close. So we'll take a path near the old house and start looking there."

Joey led the way. After they had gone a short distance, they straddled a fallen tree in the trail. They trotted on with last year's leaves crunching under their feet. Presently they came to a small clearing dotted with wild flowers. Vicki got down on her knees and buried her face in a cluster of daisies. She was about to pick some when she heard Tim exclaim, "Look what I found!"

Vicki came running and discovered the boys examining the cast-off antlers of a deer.

"Wow!" cried Joey, shaking his head in amazement. "I've hunted for antlers for months!"

"Oooh." Vicki bent down to touch the antlers. "I wonder what made them fall off."

"Male deer shed their antlers in the spring. They grow them back."

"What for?"

"Bucks fight other bucks in the fall. You should see them bang their antlers together!"

36

"Why don't you keep these, Joey?" Tim offered.

Joey's face lit up, but he hesitated. "Are you sure?"

Tim nodded.

Joey took the antlers and carefully laid them by a tree. "I'll get them on the way back. These antlers are going to hang in my room, and when I look at them, I'll remember looking for the meteorite," said Joey.

Tim said only, "It won't be such a good memory if we don't find it."

For the next half hour, he and his friends looked around the marsh and the neighboring area. They searched behind logs and large boulders covered with moss. But there was no sign of the meteorite, and Tim and Vicki were getting discouraged. With long faces they walked slowly past some tree stumps.

Joey frowned as he looked at his friends. "You give up so easy. We've got lots more places to look for the meteorite on this island. Why don't we go back to the old house where we heard the crash? Maybe we can figure out where the fireball fell."

Tim and Vicki trailed behind him, along a deer path that went by boulders that stood like sentinels among the ferns.

The children trudged on and after going a few more yards they saw the old house. The windows were dark and the branches of a nearby tree creaked in the wind.

Tim and Vicki hesitated.

"I'm going to try the front door again," Joey announced. He started walking up the four rickety steps to the porch.

Tim and Vicki followed. In silence they watched Joey give the doorknob a good twist and then jump back in alarm.

"The lock's broken," he whispered. "Someone has been in here."

"What do we do now?"

"I think we'd better go," Vicki said.

"I don't." Tim tried to push open the door, but it wouldn't budge. "Come on, Joey. Give me a hand."

"But I don't think it's safe to go inside," Joey whispered. "Do you?"

Tim said, "I don't know." His legs were trembling, but he told himself he must be brave. After all, he was looking for his telescope, and if he was going to find it, he would have to try everywhere—even this old house. Tim pushed against the door with his shoulder.

Joey helped him, and together they managed to open the door on its squeaking hinges.

Cautiously, the boys peered inside. The hall was flooded with daylight from a rear window, and there were footprints on the dusty floor.

"What do you see?" whispered Vicki. She looked ready to run at a second's notice.

"Someone has been in this house, all right. There are tracks all over the place," Tim whispered back.

"And I don't think we should go any farther,"

added Joey. "It could be dangerous. I wish Sheriff Williams was here."

"I do too," Tim admitted. Then once again his missing telescope loomed up in his thoughts, and he heard himself say, "I'm going to search this house—even if I have to do it alone."

"I'll go with you." Joey's voice sounded small. With clenched fists, he tiptoed down the hall in back of Tim. Next came Vicki, and even she was scared.

Then, with wildly beating hearts, the children looked in the living room. To their relief they saw only strips of wallpaper on the floor. They looked in the bedroom. First Tim, then Joey and then Vicki peered into the room. They all gasped as they stared at tracks leading to a closet with the door partly open.

"Let's get out of here," whispered Joey. "I don't want to see what's inside that closet."

"I don't either," whispered Vicki. "We might never come out!"

Tim swallowed hard as he stared at the closet. He looked at Joey who was white with fright. With a determined expression, Tim went and pulled the closet door wide open. He drew back, ready to run, but nothing happened. So he looked inside.

"Aw, there's only some old clothes hanging in here."

Joey stuck his head in and made the same comment.

"Yes," Vicki said. "But the tracks go in here and they don't go out."

"You *are* right about the tracks," Joey said, moving

away from the door. "Someone could be in there right now."

Shakily, Tim pushed past the clothes and stepped into the closet. He was feeling along the walls when he nearly lost his footing.

"Look!" he cried, and they peered into the closet. He was kneeling in front of an opening in the floor.

"This leads to a crawl space under the house," he explained, his voice rising with excitement. "When I pulled back this carpet, I found a cover over this hole. Once dad and I crawled in the space under our old house. We couldn't stand up. So we just crawled along. I'm going down and see what's under this house."

"I don't think you should, Tim," Vicki said.

Jocy looked into the dark hole and shuddered. "If you go down there, Tim, you're braver than I am."

That was all Tim needed to hear. He lowered himself through the opening and onto the ground under the house. He crawled a few yards and groped around with his hands because the area was darker than he had expected. But he wasn't afraid of the dark, he told himself. Last night had proven that.

Tim crept along the ground a few yards more, still feeling around with his hands. Suddenly he uttered a shrill cry. A lizard had slithered up close to him.

Joey and Vicki heard him scream.

"Tim!" shouted Joey. "Are you all right?"

"Tim! Come out!" yelled Vicki.

Tim did not answer. He moved backwards in a zigzag fashion and then stopped in alarm. His foot had jammed against a hard object. Was it a gun?

Goose pimples ran up and down Tim's spine as he turned and cautiously felt behind him. Then he burst into a joyous cry. "My telescope! I found my telescope!"

Joey and Vicki could hardly believe their ears. But when Tim hoisted the instrument through the opening, Joey grabbed the telescope and held it as if it were his own.

Vicki also laid a loving hand on the instrument, and hugged her brother after he had climbed out of the opening. "I was sure someone was going to kill you," she said.

Tim tried to make nothing of his experience. "There was no one down there," he said in an offhand voice. "I'm going back and look for the meteorite."

"Oh, no, Tim! Don't go," pleaded Vicki.

"She's right," said Joey. "It's not safe down there. Besides, the meteorite must be pretty big from the noise it made when it landed on the island. So a person would have a heck of a time fitting it through this hole."

Tim thought a moment. "I guess you're right. I would have bumped into the meteorite if it was there." After a pause he added, "What I can't figure out is why someone hid my telescope under this house. It doesn't make sense to me."

"And why was there only one set of tracks?" said Joey.

42

"There must be another way out of the crawl space," said Tim. "Whoever did it must have been trying to spook us."

"Maybe the red-haired man doesn't want us to come out here tonight," suggested Vicki. "He's probably going to look for the meteorite when nobody is around, and if we are on the island, we'd interfere with his plans."

Joey snapped his fingers. "You're smart to think of that. I'll bet it is the red-haired man."

Tim agreed. "I'm sure it is. So we've just got to find the meteorite before he does." Tim looked at his wristwatch. "Gosh! It's almost twelve o'clock, Vicki. We've got to get back. Mom doesn't like it if we're late for lunch."

"Neither does my mom," said Joey. "We'll come back this afternoon."

CHAPTER FIVE

The Fingerprints

SEVERAL DAYS had passed since the telescope had been found. The children had hunted on the island for the meteorite and they had stargazed and kept on the lookout for the red-haired man, but he had not shown up. In fact, they had not seen him since the day he had asked them to get a tow for his boat. No one else showed any interest in the island or seemed to have seen the fireball streak across the sky.

Tim was very discouraged now. He felt certain that the red-haired man had found the meteorite and was keeping it a secret because he knew that it belonged to the owner of the island. Vicki was of the same opinion. Joey felt that they should continue the search, and he urged his friends to go to the island again that morning.

As they hurried out onto the dock, they saw Skipper and Ronnie talking near the rowboat. They had their fishing rods and were examining them carefully.

Skipper smiled when he saw Joey and the others coming toward them. "How are you doing?" he asked them.

Before Joey could answer, Sam came up and greeted him with a big smile. "Where have you and your friends been keeping yourselves? I haven't seen you in days."

"Oh, we've just been fooling around, Sam," Joey answered.

"You mean you haven't found who was flashing the strange lights on the island the other night?" asked Skipper, giving Joey a playful jab in the ribs.

"Strange lights on the island!" exclaimed Sam. "So that's what you children have been keeping a secret."

Joey squirmed and looked the other way. He didn't want to answer any more questions.

"They certainly were scary. Weren't they, Ronnie?" said Skipper.

His cousin nodded.

"Cowards!" Sam growled. "Those lights aren't half as scary as some of the other things I've seen on that island."

The children were silent.

"What other things, Sam?" Joey ventured.

Sam looked around to see if anyone else were listening. Then he leaned forward and whispered, "Lots of things. Like—" he paused for effect—"giant insects."

Vicki recovered first. "Giant insects?"

"Yep," Sam nodded. "Ladybugs as big as one of them Volkswagen cars. Why do you think they call those things 'Beetles'?"

Vicki started to giggle.

"Oh, come on, Sam!" Joey cried.

Sam chuckled. "Well, I guess I'll move along and do some fishing and leave you kids to your secrets." With that he winked, turned on his heel and walked away.

"We've got to go," Skipper announced, "We have important things to do."

"You're not the only one," Vicki said. Tim jabbed her in the side, but Skipper and Ronnie were already sauntering away.

Tim looked at Vicki and sighed with relief. "I was afraid Skipper was going to ask more questions about the island and you would give it all away."

Vicki scowled. "Why, I haven't even told Mother about the meteorite. She'd never let us look for it if she knew what's happened on the island since we came here. There are those mysterious lights, almost losing your telescope, and then the fireball!"

"Shhh! Not so loud!" Tim looked around uneasily. But there was no one in sight. So he walked toward their canoe and stopped short.

"Hey!" he yelled. "Come here quick!"

46

In a few seconds Vicki and Joey were at his side. "What's up?" said Joey.

"Don't you notice something different?" asked Tim.

Vicki tilted her head, looked at the canoe and then said slowly, "Didn't we leave the canoe next to that post over there?"

Tim nodded. "Someone must have used it last night. Why else would they move it?"

Vicki kneeled and looked carefully into the canoe. Suddenly she drew her breath in. "Hey, Tim. Look at the paddles."

Tim kneeled beside her, and pulled the two paddles out from under the seat.

"We stuck them in front, and now they're under the back seat," Vicki explained.

Tim was turning the paddles over. "That's not all. Both of them are caked with mud. I know for a fact the paddles were clean last time we used the canoe."

Vicki took one of the paddles. "So what does this mean?"

"It means someone used our canoe last night—two people in fact."

Joey jumped up. He had an idea. "Wait! Put the paddles down, and don't touch them until I say! I'll be back before you can count fifty."

Tim and Vicki looked at their friend in amazement. "What are you going to do?" Vicki asked him.

"You'll see," Joey replied. He was off like a streak.

47

True to his promise he returned a few minutes later. He had a roll of scotch tape, a can of talcum powder, a magnifying glass, and gloves on his hands.

"I'm going to take the fingerprints on the oars," he announced. "Talcum powder will do the trick."

Tim and Vicki watched Joey dust one of the paddle handles with powder. Carefully, he pressed a piece of tape on a fingerprint. He pulled off the tape with the print on it. Then to protect the powder, he stuck another piece of tape on top of the print. He did this a few times. After about ten minutes he began studying the prints through the magnifying glass.

"Man! Look at this thumbprint!" he cried. "The person cut his finger. You can see the scar in the print."

Tim and Vicki took turns looking through the magnifier. They were amazed at the many fine lines they saw in the print, and the clearly visible scar.

"Do you know anyone with a scar on his thumb?" asked Tim.

Joey thought a moment. "Nope. But sometimes people walk along the dock and look at our floating houses—any one of them could have taken your canoe."

"But what about the red-haired man?" asked Tim. "He could have a scar on his thumb."

"That's true. Let's take prints on the other paddle and see what we get." Joey did so, carefully following the same procedure.

48

"Well," he concluded, "there are other thumbprints here, but nothing with a scar."

"That just proves our point!" cried Tim. "Two people used our boat last night."

"The question is—who? If it's the red-haired man, who's helping him?"

"Didn't he say he had a friend to meet? Remember?" Vicki exclaimed. "When we first met him he told us to hurry up because he had to meet someone. Maybe *that's* his assistant. Maybe they're both looking for the meteorite and his boat conked out so he used our canoe to go to the island."

"Well," Joey said, "even if it is them, there's no reason to think they went to the island. Maybe they were just paddling around in the river."

Vicki shrugged. Then her eyes caught something else in the canoe. It was a brown pellet from a great horned owl. Vicki climbed into the canoe, picked up the pellet and showed it to the boys.

"A great horned owl's pellet!" cried Joey. "That proves that whoever used your canoe went to the island. Great horned owls don't like to be where people live. The island is the only place around here where you find these. So this pellet is a great clue. The person who found it on the island must have left it in the boat. It's lucky you spotted it, Vicki."

Vicki's eyes sparkled. "Maybe we're on to something," she said.

Tim was wondering how they were going to track

49

down the culprit. But, before he could express his thoughts aloud, lightning flashed in the sky and several claps of thunder boomed overhead. Then came large drops of rain.

"Now Mom won't let us go to the island," wailed Vicki. "What about the meteorite?"

Tim frowned. "Don't talk so loud, Vicki. Do you want everyone to hear?"

Vicki's eyes flashed with anger. "There's no one here except us," she snapped. "So just calm down and quit ordering me around."

Tim looked at his sister in surprise.

Then his face fell. "Now we've got to wait until tomorrow to look," he said. "And by that time whoever used our canoe will probably use it again and go to the island." He turned and walked toward the house.

Joey and Vicki watched him in silence. Then they followed him.

CHAPTER SIX

The Tape Recorder

TIM LEANED on the windowsill and watched the rain splash on the river. For two days and two nights he had not been able to go to the island. He was more afraid than ever that someone had found the meteorite. The world outside looked as gray and glum as he felt inside.

He didn't even have Vicki for company. She had closed herself in her room and was putting the finishing touches on a plastic model of the *Enterprise* space shuttle. She said she wanted to get a feel for it before she went to the moon for her fifteenth birthday. She was even saving up for a ticket.

Just then Vicki burst into the room. She was smiling. "What are *you* so happy about?" Tim muttered.

51

"I finished my model and the weatherman predicts 'Fair' tonight and tomorrow. We can probably go to the island after dinner."

Tim jumped up from the sofa and swung his sister in the air. "Great! At last!"

A few moments later a familiar whistle outside brought Tim and his sister to the back door.

Joey was carrying a package. "The weatherman says—"

"We know," Tim and Vicki answered together. "What's that?"

"Grandma sent me a tape recorder! Now I can record the noises the animals make when we go to the island tonight. I'll bring it."

He added, "Mom made me promise to leave by ten o'clock. It gets dark by nine-thirty, but I can record some sounds before that."

"And we've got a lot of other things to do," added Tim. "I'd like to find out just how valuable a meteorite is."

"How do we do *that*?" Joey inquired.

"We'll call the science department at the university. They're sure to have an observatory, or at least someone who knows something."

Joey and Vicki watched while Tim dialed information, wrote down the university's phone number, dialed again, and then waited for ten minutes for a scientist to come to the phone.

52

"They had to get him out of the lab," Tim whispered to Vicki and Joey. At last he heard a voice. "Hello? Yes, my name is Tim Andrews, and I'm . . . doing a report on meteors. I was wondering how valuable a meteorite is?"

Tim listened, and then suddenly motioned for a pencil. Vicki ran to the kitchen and brought him one. He started scribbling. "Some are worth about ten dollars a gram? A gram—" he hesitated. "Well, I don't *exactly* know . . ." He listened for a few more minutes. Finally, nodding, he said, "Thank you very much. You've been a big help."

He hung up the phone and turned to Joey and his sister.

"Well?" Vicki urged. "Tell us! How much is it worth?"

"We don't know *yet*. It could be a lot or it could be nothing. It depends on the size and what's in it. He says a meteorite with diamonds or copper in it would be priceless. But those are very rare. Sometimes they disintegrate when they hit the ground, or splatter all over the place, or are made of 'lunar material' and then they aren't worth much."

"Lunar material?" echoed Joey.

"From the moon," Tim answered briefly. "Well—"

The three children were speechless.

"We've *got* to find the meteorite," Tim concluded.

The first thing they did when they reached the island after dinner was to hunt for the meteorite. They searched behind the old house and the surrounding area. They sloshed through puddles and left footprints in the mud. They even looked at the marsh, hoping to see part of the meteorite exposed in the soft wet soil. But it was getting dark, and searching was difficult. Tim was almost beside himself with worry.

He put his hand to his cheek and said, "I'm dead sure now that either someone has found it, or it's disintegrated."

"Well I'm not." Joey looked very determined. He paused and then announced, "My hunch is that it fell near the end of this island. It's too late to look for it now. But we can still spy on animals tonight."

"Oh, all right," Tim said reluctantly. "How do you spy on animals?"

"I read this book that says we have to rub some wild mint on our hands and clothes to hide our human scent."

Tim and Vicki did as Joey suggested. Then they all put on the masks that Joey had brought along. They were made out of Joey's mother's old dark stockings.

The children stared at each other, laughing and joking about how funny they looked.

Joey lowered his voice. "The animals sure won't see our faces when they're covered like this," he said. "And I put red paper over my flashlight because night animals are not afraid of red lights. Let's set up the telescope and I'll record some animal sounds while we're stargazing." He removed his mask.

Tim and Vicki also took off their masks and trotted with their friend to the stargazing grounds. Tim set up his telescope, and Joey recorded the chirping song of a cricket. "The insect makes noise by scraping one wing across the edge of the other," said Joey. Then he recorded the rustling noise of the leaves made by the wind.

"You're getting lots of night sounds, Joey," remarked Vicki.

"Shh!" he said. "The recorder will pick up your voice and interfere with the other sounds."

Vicki nodded to show she understood. She didn't utter another word, but she giggled when a bullfrog croaked and Joey croaked back.

After that Joey turned off the recorder and went to see what Tim was looking at through the telescope. It was the planet Saturn.

"Saturn has nine moons," Tim explained. "And it has three bright rings around it. It's a beautiful planet."

Joey stared at the brilliant rings through the telescope. "Man! That's something. The rings are what makes Saturn famous, right?"

"Right," answered Tim. "Also, it's the second largest planet."

Vicki also had to see Saturn's rings through the

telescope. "Oooh!" she sighed. "They're beautiful. I'd love to go there."

Tim adjusted the telescope and looked through it once more. "Someday," he said, still looking through the telescope, "I hope to discover a new comet. A Japanese boy discovered one. It's named after him. And . . ."

Tim did not finish, for just then a bird hooted: "Oot-too-hoo, hoo-hoo!"

"A great horned owl!" cried Joey. "Remember? I told you that when he hoots it sounds spooky."

Vicki nodded. "Can we see it?" she asked.

"We might," Joey replied. "Let's put on our masks and sit here real quiet."

In a few seconds the children had on their masks. They waited. Soon another sound broke the stillness of the night.

"A coyote howling," whispered Joey. "He sounds real close, too. I saw a coyote on this island a while ago."

Suddenly a rustling noise in the nearby brush caught their attention. They had their flashlights ready, focused on the bushes. A second later a black-furred animal with two broad white stripes down his back came out into the open. "It's a skunk," whispered Joey. "Don't move."

The animal looked around and slowly waddled in their direction.

The children held still as statues. Vicki did not even

blink an eyelid. Soon another animal came into view. It was a young coyote with yellowish gray fur. It moved toward the skunk and began circling it.

Immediately the skunk lowered his head and arched his back. Then he thumped on the ground with his forefeet to let the coyote know he'd better not come a step further.

The coyote paid no attention to the skunk's warning. He moved forward.

The skunk stamped again—this time in anger.

Still the coyote advanced.

Then the skunk raised his broad-plumed tail. He turned his back and sprayed liquid in the coyote's face.

Yelping, the coyote started for the river to bathe his eyes. He had been gone only a second when a creature with enormous wings flew over the skunk. It was a great horned owl. Joey couldn't help exclaiming.

The large bird swooped downward, silent as a shadow, and grabbed the skunk in its talons. Then the owl flew off with its victim, as quietly as it came.

The smell of skunk filled the air. The children took off their masks, and holding their noses, started to run—Joey with his tape recorder, and Tim with his telescope. In a few minutes, they launched the canoe and Tim and Vicki paddled for home.

"Boy! I sure could think of better things to smell than a skunk," said Tim.

Vicki giggled. "So could I."

When they reached shore, Joey heard a nighthawk flying overhead. It was calling *beep, beep, beep* and catching insects on the wing.

"I'm going to record the nighthawk," Joey announced as they moored the canoe. "I always hear that bird at night before I go to sleep. It's a strange call, don't you think?"

"It's nicer than the great horned owl," said Vicki.

They waited quietly while Joey recorded the hawk.

"Joey," Tim said suddenly.

"Shhh!" Joey hissed. "You'll ruin it!"

"No, listen, I just thought of something. Something that may help us find the meteorite."

Scowling, Joey switched off the recorder. "What is it?"

"If we can spy on animals, why can't we spy on human beings?"

"What do you mean?" Joey still looked angry.

"I mean—record someone."

"I get it!" Vicki chimed in. "We hide here and record the red-haired man when he comes to use our canoe."

Just then Joey heard the loud bell his mother rang when she wanted him.

"Uh-oh, there's my signal. No way I can stay out tonight and record anything—"

"But tomorrow might be too late." Tim said.

"Can we leave the recorder here? Hide it some-where?" Vicki suggested. "How long does it work?"

"Each side of the tape is sixty minutes." Joey seemed to be thinking the idea over. "I guess we can. It shuts off by itself."

"We can hide it under this pile of rope by the canoe."

The bell sounded again. "I've got to go!" Joey exclaimed. Quickly he pulled a cassette out of his pocket, placed it in the recorder, and shoved it under the rope. "There! Now let's just hope the red-haired man or whoever it is comes in the next hour and . . . and says something! If I don't get home fast, I'll be grounded tomorrow."

"We'll be in trouble ourselves," Tim admitted. "It's probably 10 o'clock already."

Joey waved to them and was off, running quickly toward home.

Vicki and Tim hurried home, too.

"I was about to call the sheriff," said Mrs. Andrews.

"We're sorry, Mom," said Tim. "We were stargazing and watching the animals and forgot the time."

"We're really sorry," added Vicki, reaching up and giving her mother a kiss. "Honest, we are."

Mrs. Andrews tried to look stern. "Well, just see that it doesn't happen again."

Tim and Vicki nodded solemnly and headed for bed.

60

CHAPTER SEVEN

The Secret Meeting

THE NEXT MORNING, Tim and Vicki sat impatiently through a visit to the dentist. They squirmed in their seats, anxious to check on Joey's tape recorder. When they finally got home, it was almost noon. They rushed through their lunch, and just as they were setting off for Joey's house, the telephone rang.

While Tim hurried to answer it, Vicki waited impatiently for him at the door.

"It's Joey," he said to her. "He sounds excited. What did you say, Joey? I was talking to my sister ... As a matter of fact, we were just on our way over to your house ... Wow! We'll be right over."

Tim hung up and looked at his sister. "Joey's tape recorder picked up something. Let's get over there fast!"

61

Tim and Vicki rushed out the back door. Across the bridge and down the dock they ran. They almost bumped into Fred Emmett and excused themselves, then dashed on and collided with Skipper. He dropped his fishing tackle and can of worms.

"What's your big hurry?" he yelled.

"Yeah. Why don't you watch where you're going?" added Ronnie, who was with Skipper.

Tim and Vicki turned red in the face. "We're sorry," they apologized.

· They helped Skipper gather his things together. Tim took care of the worms and saw that they were back in the can. Vicki picked up the fishing tackle and handed it to Skipper.

He glared at her in silence and then walked on with Ronnie.

"Golly, Skipper sure was mad," whispered Vicki.

"It was just an accident," Tim protested.

Then she and Tim hurried down the dock to Joey's. When they reached his house, they were out of breath. He was waiting for them at the back door.

"Mom went shopping," he greeted them. "So I thought we would hold a secret meeting in my room."

"What goes?" asked Tim, following his friend into the house with Vicki. "Has anyone found the meteorite?"

"Not exactly," Joey hedged.

Tim was getting impatient. "Well, what happened?"

"I played the tape back, and I think you should

listen to it," Joey said simply, opening his door. "Don't mind the stuff and things all over the place. Mom tells everyone that my room looks like a museum, but she lets me do what I want as long as I keep it clean."

Vicki looked around in amazement. She had never seen a room like it. All sorts of nature books lay on his desk and chairs. Bird feathers and several nests decorated his bureau. A stuffed owl and an old hornets' nest were on a table by the window.

Vicki was entranced with the owl. She ran her fingers over its soft feathers and examined its glassy eyes.

Tim was interested in the hornets' nest, which was shaped like a football. "Where did you find this?" he asked Joey.

In one breath, Joey said, "I climbed up a tree on the island last winter and pulled it off a branch. The nest was deserted."

Tim fingered the nest walls.

"It looks like paper," he said.

"It is!" Joey exclaimed. "The hornets bite off bits of soft wood from a tree or a house. Then they chew the wood and mix it with saliva in their mouths and—presto—the wood becomes paper!"

Tim shook his head in astonishment. "You mean they made paper before people did!"

"Yeah!" Joey said. "Isn't that weird?"

Joey walked to his dresser and pulled open his bureau drawer. Tucked among his underwear was the milky-white skin from a black snake.

Joey proudly dangled the skin in front of Vicki. "This snake skin won't hurt you, scaredy cat," he said to her. "I found it last spring. A black snake had shed his skin when it got too tight for him."

Vicki showed no interest. "Go away with your old snake skin," she said with a toss of her head. "And play the tape for us!"

"Yeah, what *about* this secret meeting?" asked Tim, shaking an accusing finger at his friend. "We can look around your room anytime."

"All right, all right."

Joey closed the door. Then he walked to the window and closed it, too. He also drew the blind, putting the room in semi-darkness.

Tim and Vicki looked at Joey, puzzled. They shrugged and waited anxiously to see what he was going to do next.

Joey cleared his throat and said in a low voice, "I want to be sure that no one else hears what you are about to hear."

Tim could not stand the suspense any longer. "Well, hurry up and tell us what it is," he said.

"Don't be so impatient," Joey answered. He went and picked up the tape recorder on his desk and then solemnly turned it on.

Tim and Vicki listened. But they could hear nothing. Then came the night sounds Joey recorded on the island.

"Keep listening," said Joey. "It's coming. And it's

going to give you goose pimples."

Tim shifted uneasily from one foot to the other. Vicki stood as still as a statue and held her breath. But all that came from the microphone were some cries from the nighthawk and the noise of a speedboat going by. After that there was the far-away bark of a dog, and a cat meowing on the dock.

Tim shook his fist at Joey in disgust. "Stop your fooling. I thought we were going to hear something exciting."

"You are," he answered. "I told you to be patient."

More night sounds came from the microphone as the recorder continued playing.

Joey listened intently. Suddenly he held up his hand. "Here it comes. Take in every word because it's a good clue."

Just then a voice came from the microphone.

"It's almost an hour since they went in. Can't we take their canoe now?"

"All right. If only mine hadn't sprung a leak! That boat's a real lemon . . . Be careful. Have you got everything?"

"It's all here."

"Good."

There were sounds of the two men getting into the canoe. The first voice started again.

"This was perfect timing. Now should be just the right time to look around without anyone knowing. If everything goes okay, we can go to the marsh this time tomorrow night, too."

"Probably." There was a pause, then the second voice added, "I bet we can make a mint off this if we handle it right. Get in the newspapers and everything."

"Oh sure. They'll make a big fuss about it."

After that there was the sound of bottles being opened, followed by silence. The tape on the recorder had run out.

"Now what do you think?" asked Joey, looking at his friend with a pleased grin. "Isn't that some clue?"

Tim shook his head. He could hardly believe what he had just heard. He asked Joey to play back the tape so that he could listen to every single word.

Joey was glad to fill his friend's request. They listened carefully to a re-play of what the two people had said on the dock.

Tim was still shaking his head in astonishment. "I'm sure glad you have a tape recorder."

Joey sighed. "I don't recognize the voices."

Tim didn't either. "But we've got a good clue here. There's no doubt now that two people are after the meteorite and know it's valuable. Maybe they found it and hid it in the marsh. I'll bet it's the red-haired man and that friend of his."

"Well, what are we waiting for?" asked Joey. "We've searched around the marsh, but there must be some place we've overlooked. So the sooner we get back there, the better."

CHAPTER EIGHT

More Evidence

AFTER THEIR SECRET MEETING, the three of them set out for the island, with Tim and Joey paddling as fast as they could. But no sooner had they carried the canoe ashore than Tim stared aghast at two different kinds of fresh footprints on a nearby sandbar.

Vicki saw them too and pointed them out to Joey. "They've been here!" she whispered. "Maybe they're still here and they're hiding in the brush or in those tall plants around the marsh."

"Then let's go there," said Tim.

He led the way. Vicki and Joey followed.

But when they reached the marsh, they could see no crouched figures hiding in the tall grass.

"You know something?" said Tim. "The men aren't

here now because we probably would have seen a boat moored on the sandbar."

"You're right," said Vicki. "Besides, they've been using our canoe. The footprints must be from last night."

Joey spoke up. "But where in thunderation is the meteorite? If it landed in the marsh, we'd see it in the shallow water."

"Maybe not," Tim said. "It could sink down in the mud and the water would cover it." He sighed.

"Then why are those men coming to the marsh tonight?" asked Vicki. After a slight pause she answered her own question. "Maybe they're going to wade in the shallow water and look for the meteorite."

"That's it!" said Joey.

"Why don't we look in the water right now?" Tim suggested, his eyes brightening.

Joey hesitated. "I don't think we should. That mud is almost like quicksand. We would sink in, and then we'd be in trouble."

Tim's rising hopes of finding the meteorite had quickly faded. Looking downcast, he sat on a log and cupped his chin in his hands. Joey and Vicki did the same.

For several minutes nobody said anything. Then Vicki, in a hushed whisper, pointed out a great blue heron that had just landed along the shore. It was a large bird with a slate-blue body and long toothpick legs.

The heron lifted one foot in slow motion, then the other as it inched through the shallow water, looking for food. Its keen eyes soon spotted a ripple on the water. Quick as a flash the heron jabbed with its beak and snapped up a tiny fish.

Vicki got up and walked over to some cattails. Anxiously, she peered between the tall plants, hoping to catch a glimpse of the meteorite, but all she saw were a few tiny fish scooting about in the shallows. So she started back to join the boys who were still sitting on the log.

She had gone only a few yards when her eyes rested on a brightly colored object near some plants. Quickly, she bent down. It was an empty box of film.

"Now why didn't I see this before?" she muttered to herself. Slipping the box in her pocket, she went on when something else caught her attention—two empty bottles.

Just as she was about to pick them up, Joey came to see what she was looking at. "Hey! Don't touch those!" he shrieked.

Vicki jumped. "Golly! You scared me, Joey. Why didn't you let me know you were coming?"

Joey didn't answer. He pulled a soiled handkerchief out of his pocket and carefully wrapped it around one of the pop bottles. "Have you got a handkerchief?" he asked Vicki.

She shook her head. "I know what you're going to do—take the fingerprints on that bottle."

"Right. But I need another handkerchief for this other pop bottle so that I don't get my own fingerprints on it."

By this time Tim was at his side—all excited. "Wow! You found some more clues."

Vicki quickly corrected him. "You mean I did. And I found something else too." She pulled the empty film box out of her pocket and showed it to the boys. "Somebody has been taking pictures here," she said.

"I'll say they have," said Tim. "Now why would someone take pictures of the marsh?"

Joey shrugged. "You got me, but how am I going to get this other bottle back to my house without my fingerprints on it?"

Tim thought a moment and then looked down at his jeans which were cut off above the knees. He tore off a piece and gave it to Joey.

"Mom said these jeans are ready for the trash can."

Joey grinned and carefully wrapped the material around the other bottle, gave it to Vicki to carry, and then the three of them hurried toward the sandbar. Soon they were in the canoe and paddling back to shore.

A short while after that they were in Joey's room, waiting breathlessly while he took the fingerprints from one of the pop bottles. They were disappointed, though, when the magnifying glass showed no thumbprint with a scar. But after the other bottle was fingerprinted, they all looked through the magnifier a second time, and there, clear as day, was the scar thumbprint they were after.

Joey was so excited that he could not stand still. "This fingerprint proves more than ever that the person who used your canoe took it to the island." Vicki was thinking. "Aren't the two men whose voices you recorded coming to the marsh tonight?" she asked.

Tim sighed and then groaned.

Joey and Vicki looked at him in alarm. "Are you all right?" Vicki asked.

"Sure. Don't mind me," he answered. "I was just thinking that we haven't come any closer to finding the meteorite since it fell on the island."

"We have too," Joey said. "We know the marsh has something to do with it."

They were silent a moment.

Suddenly Vicki cried out: "I know what we should do. We should spy on the men tonight. Then we can tell where the meteorite is."

"That's an idea!" Joey said.

"But I don't think we should use our canoe," said Tim. "If we do, the guys won't come to the island, and then we can't spy on them."

Joey agreed and looked thoughtful.

"I know what we can do!" Vicki clapped her hands. "We can use your father's boat, Joey, and we can hide it in the bushes on the sandbar so that the men won't see it."

"Yeah, that's right. The old tub is good for some-

thing, after all. Okay. I'm all for spying on the men. It should be more exciting than spying on the animals. And I bet we'll find the meteorite. If the men go off with it, we'll trail them and we'll get Sheriff Williams. So they won't go very far, Tim."

Tim looked hopeful—more so than he had in days.

CHAPTER NINE

Lumps of Earth

AFTER DINNER they hurried along the dock of floating houses. They were excited and very much disturbed. Joey's father's boat was missing.

"We've just got to find your dad's boat, Joey," said Vicki. "Or how will we spy on the men?"

"I know," Joey mumbled as he looked anxiously at the different craft tied to the dock.

Tim was the most upset of all because he was certain the men were going to haul the meteorite away tonight, and they wouldn't be able to track them down. The meteorite could be lost forever.

Then Joey said, "Let's go to the marina and see if my dad's boat is there."

In no time the three of them were at the marina. Ducks were swimming around the moored boats and gulls flew here and there, dropping down and disturbing the ripples on the water made from the wind.

Vicki did not stop to look at the ducks. Instead, she ran ahead, her keen eyes searching for an old rowboat.

Finally she called out, "Is this it, Joey?"

Joey came running. "It sure is. I wonder how this old thing got here?"

"We've got a boat!" exclaimed Tim, joining Vicki and Joey a few moments later. "Now we're all set for business."

"I wish we had more time," Joey answered. "I'd like to take some more fingerprints and see if the guy with a scar on his thumb used this old tub too."

Just then Fred came up to the children. "So you've come to get your dad's old boat."

"Yeah. Do you know who left it here?" Joey asked him.

Fred shook his head. "It was here when I came to work this morning. By the way, Joey, I think you'd like to know that the red-haired man who owns that yellow and green motorboat has asked others to come to the marina and get a tow for him. Apparently the guy's motor does stall, but yesterday I told him he'd better buy himself some oars right away. We don't have time to tow him to shore every time he goes out. And do you know what he said?" Fred was gaining speed. "He said he doesn't know how to row!"

"Doesn't know how to row!" Tim echoed. Vicki giggled.

"That's right. The sheriff was getting pretty mad.

It seems this guy is vacationing here. He got the boat cheap and thought he'd do a little scouting around."

"Fred," Tim began suspiciously, "where does he do most of his scouting around? Near the island?"

Fred seemed puzzled. "He's been around the island a lot. He probably doesn't go further because his motor's always stalling."

"Thanks for the information, Fred," said Joey. "We've got important things to do on the island." He stepped into the old rowboat. Tim and Vicki followed.

Fred laughed as he watched Joey row. "You're sure going to develop muscle rowing that thing."

"I'll say," answered Joey. "It moves like a snail. But it's better than nothing. So long, Fred."

The man waved and the children waved back.

After a while Tim began to squirm on the seat of the boat. He wished Joey would try to row a little faster. "Gosh! Joey. You're taking forever to get to the island."

Joey's eyes flashed with anger. "Here, you take the oars and see how fast you can row this old tub."

Tim exchanged places and pulled at the oars, but the boat moved even slower than when Joey had rowed it.

"I'm sorry, Joey. I didn't realize how hard it was to row this."

Tim pulled with all his might on the oars. The boat glided a little faster through the water, and before long Tim reached the end of the sandbar where there were lots of bushes.

Joey looked to see if anyone was watching before they pulled the boat up on shore. "The coast is clear," he said. "There's nobody on the dock looking through binoculars, and we haven't been trailed. So let's get the boat moored."

The children pulled the boat with all their strength and soon had it hidden in some thick brush. Then they ran to the marsh and sat down on a log to wait for dark. Joey was hoping that some animals would show up. He wasn't prepared to follow them because he had left his mask at home. But he did have his tape recorder with him.

Tim was thinking of the meteorite—wondering, questioning where it could be. After a while, he got up and started wandering toward one end of the marsh. Vicki and Joey followed him. They stopped and ate some blackberries, but Tim continued tramping on and soon he picked up a deer trail. He had wanted to investigate this path before, but something had distracted him.

Presently he came to the fallen branches of several trees. He looked at them closely and then held his breath. They had been cut off cleanly.

"I wonder if the meteorite broke these branches when it crashed to the earth," he muttered to himself. He turned his head left and right, his sharp eyes tak-

77

ing in everything. He moved on a short distance and then caught his breath. There were lumps of earth strewn about.

Heart beating quickly, Tim went and pushed some brush away with his hands. His eyes brightened when he saw more fallen branches. Then his voice rang out loud and clear. "Vicki! Joey! Come quick! I found the meteorite."

Joey and Vicki just stood there, hardly able to believe their ears.

"Hurry up you guys! Come on!" Tim yelled.

Stumbling over the underbrush they hurried after him. When they reached Tim, they stood and stared open-mouthed at a hole in which the meteorite was tightly wedged. It was about the size of a basketball, irregular in shape with many smooth pits or "thumbprints" on its surface. Part of it was buried in the ground.

"I think it's an iron meteorite," Tim explained, his voice thundering with excitement. "Iron meteorites have 'thumbprints.' Stony meteorites have white specks."

Vicki was stroking the meteorite. "Just think," she said softly. "This came from outer space. This meteorite is the first thing I've ever touched from outer space!" She began digging furiously with her bare hands. And the boys joined in.

"We've got to get it out of here before those men come," said Tim. "We've just got to."

"We will," Joey assured him.

Vicki was not too sure. "How much do you think this meteorite weighs?" she asked her brother.

"About fifty pounds," he estimated.

"How are we going to get it to the boat?"

"We'll think of a way *after* we've dug it out," Tim replied.

They worked feverishly digging out the meteorite. Soon blisters formed on their fingers and their backs ached. They sat back on their heels, exhausted, but they would not give up. They dug some more until it was almost dark.

Then Joey, bleary-eyed from digging, said, "We'll never get it out. We've got to go and get help."

"Our Dad is away," said Vicki, "but he telephoned to say he'd be back tomorrow."

Tim rocked back and forth in despair. "That doesn't help us now. I'm going to stay here all night and guard this meteorite."

"You can't do that!" wailed Vicki. "Why don't we go and get Sheriff Williams?"

"Now you're talking," said Joey. "He'll help us dig it up. Come on, Tim. Let's get a move on."

Tim refused to budge. Not until his sister and Joey began pulling him along, did he consent to leave the meteorite. Then they all hurried along the deer path. When they reached the marsh, they stopped. Glowing and flickering among the grasses were strange, colored lights.

CHAPTER TEN

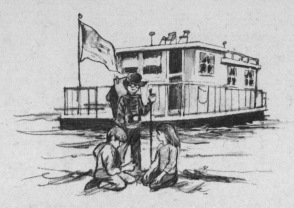

Two Dark Figures

THE LIGHTS SEEMED to be alive, even to be coming toward them. They were red, white and bluish-green—all hovering in a mysterious way but never traveling very far. Some looked like flames as they flickered over the marsh, but the brush nearby was not set afire.

"Those are the strangest lights I've ever seen," whispered Joey. "I'll bet that's what you saw the other night. They sure are spooky."

Vicki agreed. "Where could they be coming from? Do you think they're alive?"

They huddled together, watching the lights move. Suddenly Joey snapped his fingers and began to laugh. "I know what these lights are!" he exclaimed. "They're burning marsh gases. I've read about them."

"Burning marsh gases?" Tim repeated. "Now what exactly do you mean by that?"

80

"The dead stuff in swamps gives off gases that start to burn. Or sometimes lightning does it."

"They look like a thousand fireflies," said Vicki. "Are you sure they're what you said?"

"I'm sure. I think what happens is they go out in one place and light up in another which makes you think they're moving."

Joey was going to explain more about the marsh gases, but just then they heard voices.

"It's the men!" he whispered. "They've come for the meteorite. Let's duck. If they start digging around it, we'll go and get Sheriff Williams."

"All right, but where should we hide?" Tim murmured, craning his head in the direction of the voices.

"Over there in the brush," answered Joey. "Come on. Hurry up."

The three ran, stumbling, over the uneven ground, and crouched behind the brush. They sat there with their hearts pounding. The voices sounded closer. Then there was silence. A few minutes later two dark figures came into view. They were Skipper and Ronnie.

"Well, what do you know?" Tim frowned.

"I'm going to turn on my tape recorder so we'll have proof they're after the meteorite," Joey whispered.

He clicked on the tape recorder. A second later, Joey moved a cramped foot and some dry leaves crackled.

Vicki clutched Tim's arm, but Skipper and Ronnie

were so busy looking at the lights that they didn't hear the noise.

"It's up to you," Skipper was saying to Ronnie. "The weather's the best yet. If you get half-way decent pictures of these marsh gases, everyone will fall for it."

"Yeah," Ronnie said. "This batch will really do it. When I get them developed even you'll think they're flying saucers."

Vicki's mouth popped open. Furious, she tried to get to her feet but Tim held her back. Reluctantly, she sat down again and listened as the boys continued talking.

Ronnie started clicking his camera.

"Maybe I'll say a space creature came out of the saucer and spoke to me."

"No!" Skipper said. "That's too much. We'll just say we saw these weird flying saucers and got some pictures."

Skipper leaned on a tree as Ronnie took pictures from different angles. "I can see the headlines now: TEEN-AGERS SPOT UFO'S: TAKE PICTURES. Heck, Ronnie, we'll be famous!"

As Ronnie snapped the ninth photo, Vicki wrenched her arm free from her brother's grip.

Stomping loudly through the brush, she went up to Ronnie and Skipper. They jumped as if they had seen a ghost.

"What's going on?" cried Skipper. He saw two more heads pop out of the bushes. Tim and Joey came fast

on Vicki's heels, but she was already saying, "Just who do you think you are? U. F. O.'s! There are *real* U.F.O.'s and you go around pretending some marsh gases are from outer space! It's no wonder people don't believe in flying saucers! You ought to be arrested!"

"Oh come on," Skipper shouted back. "It was just a joke. Besides, we're not going to get in any trouble—you can't prove anything!"

"Oh, we have proof enough," Joey broke in. "I've got a tape recorder here that picked up every word you said."

Skipper was stunned. "Give me that tape recorder, Joey Baker!" he yelled, rushing toward him. "I'll smash your head in if you don't."

Joey struck out and kicked Skipper in the knees. The recorder slipped from his hand. Tim quickly picked it up and started running toward the sandbar.

Filled with rage, Skipper took off after Tim, shouting at the top of his lungs, "I'll get you!"

Tim kept on running. He didn't have time to turn on his flashlight, but the full moon helped to light the trail. He jumped over a log and scrambled on. Skipper was gaining on him. He tried to run faster but there was a pain in his chest and his heart was beating like a trip-hammer. Suddenly he saw a light flickering straight ahead. It came closer and the next thing he knew he ran smack into Sheriff Williams.

Skipper skidded to a stop in a cloud of sand.

84

"Sheriff!" he cried. "What are *you* doing here?"

Sheriff Williams seemed annoyed. "Towing that danged red-haired man again! 9:30 at night and I'm doing my last patrol peacefully in my boat, when all of a sudden I see a lantern waving. Same old story—his motor stalled again. I was about to give him a good lecture when I heard a lot of shouting. Now what are you kids doing here, making all that noise? Shouldn't you be home?"

"We were just playing games," Skipper said quickly. "I was racing Tim. He said he could beat me to the sandbar."

"Racing!" Tim exploded. "He was chasing me for all he was worth!"

Tim began explaining what had taken place. Just as he finished, Vicki, Joey and Ronnie caught up with them. Joey took the recorder from Tim and played back the tape. Everyone listened in silence.

When the conversation ended, Sheriff Williams' face was grim. He looked sternly at Skipper and Ronnie. "So you were planning a hoax. I heard of a man who was fined over 100 dollars after the police had investigated his hoax. The man claimed he had seen a creature from another planet, but he had taken a monkey, shaved him and cut off his tail. Now this hoax business is serious. It's fraud."

Skipper and Ronnie hung their heads. "We didn't mean any harm, Sheriff," Skipper explained. "We just wanted to have some fun."

"You mean you wanted to get your pictures and names in the newspapers," Sheriff Williams corrected them.

Skipper swallowed hard. "Well . . . er . . . yes, we did," he admitted. "But I hope we won't be fined 100 dollars, Sheriff. We don't have that kind of money."

"I'll say we don't," said Ronnie.

Sheriff Williams, still looking angry, stroked his chin thoughtfully.

Ronnie and Skipper shifted uneasily from one foot to the other, but they sighed with relief when Sheriff Williams said, "Maybe an exception can be made this time since your hoax won't appear in the paper. But see that you don't think up another one."

"We won't," they said in small voices.

Then Tim quickly spoke up. "You're the ones who hid my telescope under the old house. And you tried to scare us about the strange lights when *you* knew they were only burning marsh gases."

"We hid the telescope to keep you from stargazing. We wanted to be sure no one saw us taking the pictures," Skipper confessed. "We were going to bring it back later."

"Ronnie, do you have a scar on your thumb?" Joey changed the subject, smiling gleefully. "Did you and Skipper use Tim's canoe to go to the island?"

Joey explained how he had taken the fingerprints on the paddles. He also mentioned that the same scar thumbprint had appeared on one of the bottles that

Vicki had found in the marsh. "She also picked up a great horned owl pellet that one of you had left in the canoe," he said. "So that proved to us that someone had gone to the island because great horned owls don't like inhabited areas."

"What about the secret meeting and your tape recorder, Joey?" said Vicki, jumping up and down with excitement. "Tell them about that."

Joey lost no time relating how his tape recorder had produced evidence.

"We thought they were going to dig up the meteorite that Tim had found," finished Vicki.

"Meteorite?" Skipper said. "Here?"

Sheriff Williams smiled in amazement. "Well, I must say you kids have done some fine sleuthing. And I'm glad you caught these two culprits in the act. Now where is this meteorite? I'd like to see it."

"Yeah," said Skipper. "Me, too."

Tim, Vicki and Joey guided them all to the place where the meteorite had fallen.

Sheriff Williams could hardly believe his eyes as he examined it. "Well I'll be! A meteorite! Believe it or not, this is the first one I've seen."

"Will you help us dig it up right now?" Joey asked him.

The Sheriff laughed. "Not tonight, Joey. But I will tomorrow. Right now we'd better head home. I've still got that man to tow in, and your parents must be worried."

"The red-haired man's been waiting the whole time?"

"It serves him right," Sheriff Williams said cheerfully as they turned toward shore. Soon they were in their boats. The children stared curiously at the man, who had dozed off while waiting. Sheriff Williams shook his head, more amused than angry by this time.

The next morning there was a lot of excitement at the Andrews' floating house. Mr. Andrews had returned during the night from his business trip. At breakfast Vicki and Tim told their father every single thing that had happened while he was away.

Then Joey arrived. After eating a second breakfast, he told the story all over again, making it sound even more thrilling.

Mr. Andrews' eyes sparkled with amusement. "I'm mighty glad I bought the island. And I'm anxious to see that meteorite!"

"Sheriff Williams is going to help us dig it up," said Tim. "Do you and Mom want to come too?"

Mrs. Andrews smiled. "I can hardly believe that a meteorite fell on our island and you children have been so secretive about it. But I'll be glad to help. I've only been to the island once."

"Let's go to the Sheriff's first," Mr. Andrews suggested. "I'm sure he'll haul us all over in his 30-footer."

Mrs. Andrews packed a few sandwiches, while Mr. Andrews went to look for the strongest magnet he had. Soon the whole crew were on their way to Sheriff

Williams', who was ready for them in his boat.

It was not long before a happy group stood around the meteorite. Mr. Andrews took out his magnet and placed it on the meteorite. "Tim, I think you're right. It's probably an iron meteorite." He paused. "It could be a prize. Once we get it ashore, I'll call an authority at the university to come look at it."

Mr. Andrews was right. That afternoon a scientist examined the meteorite, which was on the deck of the Andrews' floating house, guarded jealously by Joey, Vicki and Tim. Neighbors had been stopping by all day, asking about their find. Skipper and Ronnie had been telling everyone the meteorite was three hundred pounds and solid gold.

The scientist spent about half an hour testing the meteorite with strange looking instruments. At last he was ready to give his opinion.

The first thing he said was, "You're going to make a lot of money."

"How much is it worth?" Mr. Andrews asked.

"Maybe about 100,000 dollars." He paused, viewing the shocked faces around him. "Now, that's only a rough estimate. I don't know how much a museum or university would pay for it, but it would be somewhere in that area."

"Wait a second," Tim said. "I don't want to sell it! Do you?" He turned to Vicki and Joey. "We spent so long looking for it. Why can't we keep it ourselves?"

The scientist hesitated. "It's a rare meteorite, Tim.

We could learn a lot about the solar system by studying it, and eventually apply what we learn to the national space program." He smiled at them. "I'm glad you're so interested in meteorites, and I can imagine how much time and effort you spent looking for it on your island. But I'm sure you realize that the only way we're going to learn about what's out there," and he gestured to the sky, "is to take every chance we get to study things like meteorites."

"I don't mind selling it," Vicki spoke up. "Think of all the things scientists could learn from it. And hey, Tim! You could buy a really great telescope! Then you could really discover a new comet!"

Tim's eyes brightened. The idea was tempting. And after all, if they put it in a museum, he could still go look at it. "What do *you* think, Joey?" he turned to his friend.

Joey looked down at the meteorite. "Well," he said slowly, "I sure don't have any space for it in *my* room." Tim and Vicki laughed. "Besides, I could buy a real expensive tape recorder and *really* get some great animal sounds."

"And the rest," Mr. Andrews said firmly, "goes in to your bank accounts until you're older."

"Hey," Vicki turned to Sheriff Williams. "There's *one* more thing we could buy."

"What's that?" the Sheriff asked.

"A brand new motorboat for the red-haired man!"

Tim Anderson

Stargazing List

<u>Asteroid</u>. A small planet (from about 1 mile to 500 miles wide) that travels around the sun. There are thousands of asteroids between Mars and Jupiter.

<u>Comet</u>. Looks like a star with a tail of light. A comet is made up of tiny particles in an envelope of gas. Halley's Comet returns every 77 years - so look for it in 1986.

<u>Constellation</u>. A group of bright stars that forms a pattern in the sky. There are 88 constellations.

— Big Dipper.
7 stars that form a dipper. It's part of a large constellation called Great Bear.

— Little Dipper.
Constellation shaped like a dipper but smaller than Big Dipper. At the end of

the handle is Polaris, the North Star. It guided sailors across the sea in early times.

—Leo the Lion.
A group of stars that form the shape of a lion - a sickle head and a triangle tail.

—Scorpio.
A constellation that looks like a scorpion's tail.

Fireball. A large, bright meteor.

Galaxy. A large collection of stars - there are billions of stars in a galaxy and billions of galaxies in the universe. The earth is in the Milky Way Galaxy.

Jupiter. The largest planet in our solar system. Takes 12 years to go around the sun. Has 12 moons and 3 of them are larger than our moon. Jupiter can be seen with the naked eye.

Mars. The 4th planet from the sun and the third smallest. It's called the Red Planet and looks reddish. Takes $22\frac{1}{2}$ months to go around the sun. Has 2 tiny moons.

Mercury. The smallest planet. It's closest to the sun and takes just 88 days to go around it.

Meteor. A piece of iron or stone that travels through space. Usually meteors are the size of a pea or a grain of sand. Most burn up when they hit the earth's atmosphere and this makes them glow with a bright light for a few seconds.

Meteorite. A meteor that has landed on earth in one piece or in fragments. The largest found in the U.S. weighed $15\frac{1}{2}$ tons.

Moon. A heavenly body that revolves around a planet. The earth has only one moon but

other planets have more. A moon shines by
reflecting the light of a star.

Neptune. The 4th largest planet. It takes
165 years to go around the sun. Has 2 moons.
Can't be seen with naked eye.

Planet. A large heavenly body that travels
around a star (like the sun) in a regular path.
No planet shines by its own light - it reflects
the light of its star.

Pluto. The planet farthest from the sun -
4 billion miles! It takes 250 years to
travel around the sun. No moons discovered
yet.

Saturn. The second biggest planet. It has
3 rings, 9 moons, and takes 29 years to travel
around the sun.

Solar System. The sun together with the

planets, moons, comets, meteors and everything else that revolves around it.

Star. A large globe of very hot gases that shines by its own light. Red stars are cooler than yellow stars. The hottest stars are blue-white.

Sun. Our own star — the center of our solar system. The earth and the other planets travel around it. The sun is a yellow star.

Uranus. The 3rd largest planet. It takes 84 years to go around the sun. Has 5 moons and scientists discovered that Uranus has rings around it. [Hard to see without a telescope.]

Venus. The brightest planet, and the closest to earth. It takes 224 days to travel around the sun.

Other Important Things – Added by Vicki Anderson

<u>Space Shuttle</u>. A little space ship that will carry people from Earth to a space station halfway to the moon. The first one is called the Enterprise.

<u>U.F.O.</u>-Unidentified Flying Object. Some people think they are from outer space but most of the time they turn out to be weather balloons or other regular things. But some of them might be from outer space! No one really knows.